# Terci in Chains

*A 1Night Stand Story*

**By
Kate Richards**

Copyright © 2016 by Kate Richards
ISBN: 978-1-61333-962-6
Cover art by Fiona Jayde

Published by Decadent Publishing Company, LLC
Look for us online at:
www.decadentpublishing.com

# Prologue

Terci: *So would you say an average person is born either a sub or a Dom?*

Mistress K: *I try not to rely on generalizations.*

Terci: *Okay. Then...as an example, let's go with me. We've been chatting online for a long time. I think we're friends, aren't we?*

Mistress K: *Yes, I consider you a friend.*

Terci: *Then, how about me? Would you say I have the inclination to be one or the other?*

Terci chewed her lip, waiting for the answer. Would it kill the woman to elaborate on something? Ever since the artist she'd hired to do her first indie cover had introduced her to the Domme, Terci had been both grateful and intrigued. Despite her lack of personal experience, she'd managed to write Dom/Domme and sub/slave characters her readers responded to in the most positive way. People in the BDSM community—especially Mistress K—generously helped to ensure the accuracy of her work.

And whet her appetite to learn more.

When she and Mistress K had first connected, Terci'd been in a relationship, but about eighteen months later, she and her girlfriend had parted ways. Linda claimed Terci didn't know what she wanted—and she might have been right.

But after six months on her own, Terci decided to find out if what she wrote might not be what she wanted to live. And the trip to Ottawa, Canada, for Romancing the Capital, so far from home, offered the opportunity to throw caution to the wind and test out the experience in a safe situation. 1Night Stand had come highly recommended from a girlfriend who'd met her wife through the dating service, and a hotel full of other authors offered the most secure place Terci could imagine.

According to the Website, the service arranged dates for one night only—thus the name 1Night Stand—but the testimonials from former customers swore they'd gotten more than they ever dreamed of. Many of the customers now shared the same surname.

But she didn't need marriage, so after giving

extensive personal information on the application, Terci requested a single night with a Domme, a chance to try out her fantasies. Preferably during the Canadian conference.

And a week before the event, she'd received an email confirmation of her date. Then struggled for an hour and a half with the instinct to cancel it. Would the reality be what she experienced in her dreams? Would it turn her on like her conversations with Mistress K—god, did the woman know how she affected Terci? No. If she did, the Domme would probably have stopped talking to her long ago.

Time to find out if her nerve matched her interest.

In addition to her own responsibilities at the event, her favorite author, Mariana Martin, would be attending and Terci's fan-girl side backflipped while her BDSM virgin side—anticipating her date with an unknown Domme—sent her stomach into front flips. If she didn't pull it together, she'd have a rough time presenting the calm, friendly author persona local bookstores and a few small conventions in surrounding states had experienced.

Terci Angel's *BDSM for the Non-Major* had been a hit in college bookstores across the US. Her second release, *My Dom's sub* had become a *USA Today* bestseller. Fans of her own were coming to the book signing, but Mariana's every book hit NYT without exception. Her presence ensured good attendance at the event.

Mistress K: *Terci? Are you still there?*

Terci: *Yes, Mistress. I apologize for my distraction.*

Mistress K: *I see. If you have something to do, I will say good-bye for now.*

Terci: *Okay. I have to pack for my trip anyway. I won't be on much for the next week, but I'll speak with you soon. Thanks again for your help with the collaring scene.*

Mistress K: *You're very welcome. I'm always happy to help ensure accuracy. So often the lifestyle I love is misrepresented in fiction—or in social media.*

Terci: *Good-bye, Mistress.*

Terci, in fact, had no doubt what role she'd like to try in the BDSM community, and she'd asked

Madame Eve for the Domme of her dreams. Mistress K always made her feel safe, she never chastised her in a humiliating way—rather using simple corrections in her critiques to bolster her self-esteem and guide her toward an accurate representation of the Doms and subs in real life. Always on time when they had a chat set up, she was intelligent, warm, and kind. Guiding by example—as she promised any good Dominant did.

Although Terci had no idea of her Mistress advisor's appearance—the Domme's Facebook image a scepter and flogger, crossed—she had an image in her mind, picturing her at least a few inches taller than Terci's own five-foot-two, dressed all in black leather to match her long dark-brown hair, pale skin....

But Terci hadn't asked Madame Eve for a person with a specific. She sought a Domme with a strong hand and willingness to be patient with a newbie. Although she had visited a couple of local dungeons on her own to interview participants, she'd never let her guard down enough to try...anything.

And she wanted to play, so much!

Closing the lid on her laptop, she slid it into the carry-on bag, and snapped the buckles. The taxi honked outside, and, grabbing her luggage, she hurried down to the curb.

*Canada or bust!*

# Chapter One

"Miss Martin? Miss Martin!"

Mariana finished signing her credit card slip and turned to see who was so anxious to get her attention. A youngish man with ginger hair and worried green-gold eyes bobbed up and down a few feet away from the check-in desk.

"I am so sorry I'm late. Can I take your bag? Escort you to your room?" He waved a tablet in her direction. "And I have your schedule."

Frowning at him, she asked, "Do you work for the hotel?" She arched a brow at the registration clerk, who shrugged as though to say, *I've never seen him before.*

The man's bow tie wobbled at his throat when he swallowed. If he twitched anymore, she'd go for her flogger. Anything to settle him down.

"No, no," he said. "I work for Jeanette." He paused and, when she didn't respond, plunged on. "She hurt her toe while walking her chow chow down a sidewalk after the last storm. The beast dragged her half a block before she tripped and caught her foot in a grate. Her flip-flop came right off. I told her the furry beast was too big for such a petite woman, but she and my sister bought it on their trip and...."

He babbled on while she attempted to make sense of his words. Jeanette. Her agent. Couldn't make it. A minor injury. A dog.

When he paused for breath, Terci grabbed the opportunity. "You're Phil, right? Her office assistant?" She waited until he nodded and not a second longer. "Are you sure she injured a toe? Jeanette once drove through a snowstorm with one flat tire and a bad case of the flu for a bookstore signing. She's never missed a conference, ever." And to send Phil, Jeanette's bumbling almost-brother-in-law.... His sister, Kaitlin, was her longtime partner.

"Well, she didn't want me to worry you, but they found the toe and got it on ice, and she won't be out of the reattachment surgery until later today. Jeanette is going to try to get here tomorrow if—"

Mariana dropped her suitcase. "Surgery?

Reattachment?"

He grabbed the handle and towed the wheeled bag along behind him. "You have dinner tonight with the organizers, followed by a late drink with the local booksellers. Then you'll need to get your rest because you have the contest winners' breakfast at eight and then…."

Mariana tuned him out as they stood by the elevator. She knew her schedule, but it helped to have her agent with her to keep things moving. Otherwise, she might end up chatting with the contest winners straight through lunch and miss her panels and everything else. Spending time with readers offered the cream on top of being an author.

The elevator doors opened, and they stepped inside. "Floor?" he asked.

"Six," she instructed when his hand hovered over the control panel. "Are you sure Jeanette is going to be okay? How the heck did her toe end up off her foot anyway?"

"I'm not sure. Kaitlin told me to get here and bring your files. Don't worry, Miss Martin, I can do the job.

It's my chance to prove myself." Phil consulted the tablet again. "I want to be an agent, you know."

"No, I didn't," she murmured. "How nice." The numbers lit up as they passed each floor. Finally, the car slowed. "Here's my stop." As the doors opened, Mariana moved out into the hallway and reached for her bag, but her agent's assistant held onto the handle and followed.

"It's mine, too, Miss Martin."

She sped her steps, but he clung to her side, reading aloud from the damned screen while she mentally prepared for the string of public events. "Okay, so after dinner tomorrow, you have your 1Night Stand date and then you're free until—"

The last pierced her concentration. "I beg your pardon, I don't have my agent arrange one-night stands for me. Is this a joke?"

He held the screen in front of her. "Not so far as I can tell. It's right here in your schedule."

Mariana slid the key card in and opened her door. "This had better be some kind of panel about short romances."

Phil followed her through the doorway—would the man never give up? "My notes say you should check your email." He shrugged. "That's all I know."

Unwilling to push the issue further, she set her purse and carry-on bag on a low table and sat on the couch. "If you're staying, join me."

Yanking her phone from her bag, she brought up her emails. Scanning down the list of messages, she came to one from Jeanette, subject: *Don't Kill Me.*

Oh no.

*Hi, hon! I know you're wondering WTF if Phil actually remembered to tell you about your 1Night Stand. Feel free to kill the messenger, by the way. I only keep him on because he's Kaitlin's brother, and I wouldn't have forced him on you if I'd had any options, but my pretty sweetie refused to step away from my side, and I couldn't leave you in the lurch.*

*Can you believe he thinks he's ready for his own clients? I hope he doesn't screw up too badly, and if he does, I owe you big time. He's got a good heart, you know…even if he spends his days so busy making my life hard I forget his better qualities.*

Mariana glanced at the man sitting next to her on the sofa, tapping away on his tablet, his brow furrowed in concentration. She could guide herself through a conference if she had to. Impatient to get the details of this "date," she read on.

*Okay, to get to the topic at hand before they roll me off to surgery. I wonder what would have happened if they hadn't found the toe? Would I have had to get special shoes? A prosthetic pinky toe? These drugs are really kicking my ass. Anyway, about your surprise.*

A pang of sympathy had Terci shaking her head. Toe reattachment, not to mention severing, had to be very painful.

*Your date is tomorrow night after the banquet. I'm sure you'll have a wonderful time. According to the matchmaking service, 1Night Stand, she's your dream date—at least as I envision her. Hope I'm right!*

*Super drowsy now.*

*Have a great con and maybe don't kill Phil. He may surprise us all.*

*Hugs!*

*J*

"That's it?" she muttered. "I have a date tomorrow after the dinner." She lifted her gaze to Phil. "Are you sure you don't know more about this?"

He shrugged. "Not really. I do know the service hooked her up with Kaitlin. If that helps?" He flashed her a toothy grin. "And did she tell you Katie proposed? They haven't set the date yet, but they're both floating around making goo-goo eyes at each other. I never thought I'd see my butch sister like this!"

About to protest the description, Mariana pictured Kaitlin and decided not to bother. Compared to Phil, Suzie Homemaker was butch.

"Getting married. I hadn't heard." How surprising. Jeanette should have been shouting her news from the rooftops.

"It just happened last week. She planned to share it with you this weekend, but…well, things changed."

That explains a lot." Mariana dropped her head back against the sofa cushion. "Damn couples always think everyone needs to pair up."

But why a one-night stand? If Jeanette wanted her to couple up, wouldn't she have used a traditional dating service? Or maybe she thought Mariana wasn't capable of more than one night? Insulting, but understandable. Of course, if 1Night Stand had found Kaitlin…. Mariana closed the email and glanced at the receding daylight outside the window.

"I don't have any more time to talk about this right now, Phil. I need to get ready for dinner, so either get out or find something to amuse yourself while I shower." The event wasn't the biggest all year, but one where she had many responsibilities. If Jeanette and her fiancée wanted to get her a date—why now? Their timing couldn't have been worse. As Mariana, she wrote mildly sexy and deeply emotional stories, but nothing too kinky. Her fans had no idea about her personal interests.

Phil took two steps back, probably relieved to have a break from her and the chaos to go report to his sister how things were going.

"Stop." She froze him in his tracks like a scared

rabbit. "I never play at cons. It's too risky." Her friends at her local dungeon had no idea about her pen name. Sometimes it got to be a headache being so many people. "If I am going to do this"—and she was too intrigued not to—"nobody can know who I am including my 'date.' Give me your tablet."

She opened a fresh document and typed some instructions. "I'd rather even you didn't know about this, but I have to count on you. Get that note to my date before I get to her." Her breath quickened, muscles tightening in anticipation. Her book tour had kept her from release for too long. And the long evenings Skyping with her author friend about the care and flogging of submissives and the psychology of the Doms who love them did nothing to abate her desires. In fact, she'd considered offering to make a house call for the purpose of demonstration. Only her desire to keep her alter ego separate from her author ego stopped her.

She waved aside his protestations that he didn't even know who she was meeting and fixed him with a threatening stare. "If you mess this up, I will see to it that you never represent anyone in our industry. You'll have to find a job doing promo for textbooks."

He blanched and clutched his tablet to his chest, stumbling for the door.

She found no challenge in dominating Phil. Still, he made a nice warm-up.

\*\*\*

Terci set her bag on one of the queen-size beds and surveyed her hotel room. A delay in her connection had resulted in her arrival at after three in the morning, but a lack of reasonable hours of sleep would not be enough to keep her from her morning's activities. She set her laptop on the desk and plugged it in to charge. In the nicely appointed bathroom, she washed her face and slipped into a nightie.

Her reflection showed a very tired Terci Angel. Sometimes she regretted the name, but it did seem to stick in readers' minds. Shadows under her eyes and blonde curls frizzed by the long day would have to be dealt with before she faced her public in the morning.

A quick grin at the thought brightened her face. Her public. She didn't draw the crowds Mariana Martine did. But the appearance of her favorite author would draw so many readers, everyone would benefit. She flipped off the light and headed for bed. Author or not, she'd been a reader first and had entered the contest to meet Mariana along with the rest of her fans. Starting the day at the winners' breakfast would lift her spirits, but ending it with her 1Night Stand…terrifying.

Answering the rap on the door, she accepted the pizza she'd ordered at check-in. Her healthy-eating plan went downhill fast when traveling. The only thing she'd found appealing on the short all-night menu smelled delicious, and she gobbled three pieces while lying in bed, before drifting off to sleep.

*Murky darkness surrounded Terci, so thick she couldn't push it aside. Something she had to do—something she wanted to do tickled at the edges of her brain. Exhaustion weighted her arms and legs as she sank deeper into sleep.*

*Or water, water as warm and comforting as the arms of the woman she often thought of, the basis of the Dommes in the bestsellers she penned. She sank to the very bottom of the pool of darkness and then pushed off, rising to the light of a sunny day. In the distance, traffic roared, and a train rumbled. A dog barked.*

*"Welcome, Terci."*

*The man stood outside a doorway that...glowed?*

*"Who are you?" Glancing down, she saw her form clothed in jeans and a T-shirt, low boots...her basic uniform of the day. But she'd been in a nightie a moment ago. Hadn't she?*

*"The Mistress awaits you inside." He moved to the left, and the door melted away, revealing an opening with no light whatsoever.*

*Terci stumbled into the corridor and the sunny warmth of outside disappeared, replaced by dimness. Glancing behind, she could no longer make out any opening, and she had no way to go but forward. Chill air raised goose bumps on her arms. After a dozen or so steps, she became aware of the line of light under a doorway to her left. Pressing her ear to the door, she heard a crack followed by a shriek and jerked back.*

*From another lit outline of a door, a moan, throaty and passion-filled. Another kind of torment then. Because in this place of stygian darkness, it would all be torment. As always in this dungeon.*

*How did she know?*

*The third door...silence.*

*In this dungeon, the third door was hers. Somehow, she knew that, too. Eagerness grew in her as she gripped the icy knob and turned. A single lamp in one corner dissipated the darkness.*

*"On your knees, sub."*

*The harsh tone sent her to the floor just inside the doorway. Far away, across the black-and-white tile, sat an armchair, gray herringbone-patterned and, under other circumstances, prosaic. But, in this case, the woman occupying it both terrified and tantalized her. Terci rested her palms on her thighs and straightened her back, head high, eyes cast down, in the position she always had the characters in her story take.*

*"Mistress...."*

*"Did I tell you to speak?"*

*She subsided, trembling with nerves and anticipation.*

*"Come here, on hands and knees."*

*Terci crept across the floor, placing a hand on white, a knee on a black tile until she arrived at Mistress's side. The lamp's glow tinted the floor almost shades of gray, but she knew the floor...she knew all of the room, knew mounted on the wall to her left was a two-way mirror where, if Mistress gave permission, other dungeon occupants might lurk, watching everything they did. Were they there now? At the possibility, her stomach gave a twist of excitement. To her right, a St. Andrew's cross fixed to a stand loomed far enough from the wall to allow Mistress to circle her. But the chair...the chair was new.*

*She arrived at Mistress's feet and paused, unsure what to do next. After a long moment of silence, she bent to kiss her low-heeled boot, the scent of expensive leather in her nostrils, rewarded by a hand resting on her head. Terci preened, the touch a benediction she welcomed.*

*"Have you been good?" Mistress stroked her hair in long, slow sweeps. "I have heard something disturbing."*

*Terci swallowed hard, her heart lurching with regret. She'd hoped word of her perfidy would not get to Mistress, but should have known better. "No, Mistress," she murmured. "I have not been good."*

*She moved her gaze from Mistress's legs clad in dark, slim slacks to her cream-colored tunic and up to her beloved face. Her dark hair trailed over her shoulder in a fat braid, and Terci longed to unplait it, run her fingers through its softness, hold it against her face and inhale the spicy scent that was hers alone. But, tonight, she did not deserve such pleasures.*

*Mistress shook her head, lines of sadness by her eyes. Careworn. "Domme Agatha saw you gobbling fast food burgers yesterday. Did you not ask me to help you take better care of yourself?"*

*"Yes, Mistress." Tears welled. She'd been so*

15

*happy to come, she'd pushed her behavior aside, pretending it hadn't been a big deal. "I only made one trip through the drive-through. I was running late and—" The fingers in her hair tightened and gave a sharp jerk, dragging her up off her knees.*

*"Enough excuses." Mistress's sharp tone shredded the warmth and intimacy of the moment between them. "I have better things to do than try to help someone who breaks her word the moment she leaves my sight. I should send you away."*

No! *Terci sucked a breath in and let it out in a spew of pleading. "Mistress, please no. I do need your help. I am so sorry. I know your time is valuable and you try to help me. Please, please let me try again. I need you."*

*"You need french fries and ice cream."*

*The tears spilled over and down Terci's cheeks. "No," she whispered. "I don't."*

*"Then why...did you choose them over me?"*

*"I didn't."*

*Then the hand was gone, her hair was free, and Mistress wasn't touching her at all. "You disgust me.*

*Go home, Terci, and come back when you are ready to be honest with us both."*

*She crumpled at her feet in despair. "Please. Don't give up on me."*

*"Don't you dare soak my shoes with crocodile tears."*

*Oh god. She'd waited so long for Mistress to notice her, and she finally had, a month ago, and then, the week before, with acid indigestion burning her throat and a burst of desire for self-improvement, she'd asked Mistress to help her. And how had she repaid her?*

*"Please, Mistress, please punish me."*

*Mistress pushed her away with the toe of her shoe. "I can't be bothered."*

*Terci couldn't breathe. "Please," she exhaled with the last of her air, "don't give up on me." She rubbed her sweaty hands together as long moments stretched on. It couldn't end here. "Please, I'll do anything."*

*"Stand up."*

*The bubble of pain grew so big it threatened to burst out of her chest. But she rose to her feet, head* hanging. As she began to turn away, Mistress sighed. *"First, never say you'll do* anything. *You know better. Someone else might take you up on it. What will I do with you?*

*"Jeans around your knees and bend over my lap. Let's see if we can't give you a strong-enough reminder you'll think twice before going through the drive-through again."* Mistress chuckled. *"You'll have an easier time standing in your kitchen preparing a home-cooked meal than sitting in the car stuffing your face, at least for a day or two."*

*Terci shivered, but she unbuttoned the pants, pushed them over her hips and down halfway then bent and lay over Mistress's lap, fingers braced on the floor. Her lifted arms dragged her shirt up, baring her from under her breasts to her bottom.*

*Mistress touched her hair again, softly, and trailed her palm down her back to the cleft at the top of her behind.* "So sweet, but so stubborn," she said. "I would rather spank you for pleasure, you know."

*"Yes, Mistress." Terci fought the automatic tensing preceding a punishment spanking. It would*

*hurt. Sitting would be painful afterward. She'd have to sleep on her tummy tonight. And alone. She'd not be invited home to curl up in her Mistress's arms— the worst part of the punishment.*

*The first swat hit hard on her cotton-covered fanny, and she jerked and tensed again.*

*"Breathe, Terci," Mistress said, then a flurry of slaps followed while Terci squirmed and whimpered and sniffled. "You earned this punishment, so stop writhing around before you fall on the floor and get hurt."*

*Terci tried to still herself, but when her panties were drawn down to her knees and the hard edge of Mistress's hand began to work over her bare skin, it became impossible. Hot pain peppered her buttocks and thighs. Then, nothing.*

*While she drew short gasping gulps of air, Mistress held a hairbrush under her nose. "I think this may help you remember your promises." The wide wooden back of the brush loomed menacingly before it disappeared and a forearm rested on her back. She'd have to be held in place, or she'd be sure* to cause herself harm under the pain of the hairbrush. Mistress only used it in punishment spankings and would show no mercy.

Pressing her fingers harder into the floor, Terci counted out the thudding smacks in her head. One. Two. Three. *How many more?* Five. Six. *A total of ten on her buttocks before Mistress shifted to the delicate skin of her upper thighs. She focused on breathing in and out as the pain went from a dull ache to unbearable. But she'd die before she'd be so ungrateful as to safeword when she'd earned every lick of these and more. Mistress hadn't turned her away when she'd thrown her request for help back in her face, although she could have.*

*Her world became a blur of thuds, her buttocks, her thighs, and back again until her head swam with the pain and she shivered, slipping not into subspace but into a place where she hung, suspended, waiting out the storm.*

*And then it ended, the maelstrom of spanking settled into a place of peace, and Mistress helped her sit upright on her lap and cuddled her close. Despite the ache in her abused backside, Terci rested her head against Mistress's firm, high breasts and welcomed the petting and cuddling, the kiss on her forehead.*

*"I hate that you made it necessary for me to hurt you, my Terci," she murmured. "Do you think you will be able to discipline yourself and take time to prepare and eat a healthy meal even when I am not there to remind you? Your body needs fuel to function properly."*

*She nodded. "Yes, Mistress." A haze of happiness surrounded Terci as always when in her embrace, and she'd pay any price to be there. There couldn't be another person in the world who made her feel so loved, and she hoped to one day be collared by the beautiful, elegant woman with the long, dark braid.*

*But, until then, she resolved to take every opportunity to show how much she appreciated Mistress's time and love and not to let her down.*

*"Do you hurt terribly, Terci?"*

*She snuggled closer, inhaling the warmth and wishing for more. "No, I'm fine, Mistress."*

21

*Mistress stroked Terci's hair from her face and rested her cheek on top of her head. "Would you like to come home with me tonight?"*

*Her heart lurched with happiness. "After the way I behaved?"*

*"You accepted your punishment. Let's go to my home, and I will rub some nice cream on your skin, make you some tea, and we can talk about some ideas I have to meet your goals for eating healthy without spending hours in the kitchen. It's admirable you have the desire to care for yourself better." She gave her a little shove. "Now, fix your clothes, and let's go home."*

*Home. If only they had a home together, but it was early days yet, and a Domme/sub relationship where they lived under the same roof was only a dream. But a beautiful one.*

Pepperoni, tomato sauce, garlic.... Terci forced her eyes open then wished she hadn't. The scents were accompanied by a lunar landscape of congealed cheese in a box two inches from her nose. No wonder she had food nightmares after eating half of a pizza at four in the morning. She'd been hungry, but her carry-on had held enough granola bars, peanut butter crackers, and string cheese to keep her going until breakfast. They would have been a better choice.

But hot, gooey deliciousness. And it had been very good.

She tugged the threads of the nightmare together and shook her head. The dungeon again. It bore no relation to the two she'd visited while doing research for her books. Those had been rather more ordinary, street level, one in a home on a residential street, in fact. The guardian, underground tunnel…the detail of the floor tiles behind the third door where she always went. And the chair in her dream. The upholstery bore a strong resemblance to the fabric covering the seat in the airplane the day before, so the new piece of furniture made some sense.

But the Domme never changed. Her appearance or her behavior. She behaved as Mistress K might—at least in Terci's imagination—under similar circumstances. In their long Skype conversations, her contact to the BDSM world spoke of her life as a Domme with such affection toward her subs. Mistress K protected their identities, of course, but Terci absorbed the information.

She would never meet Mistress K in person. Her tentative hints at using video Skype had been brushed aside with gentle firmness, and Terci had no idea where the other woman lived. She might not even be a woman—but if not, she certainly had the role down.

Terci's dreams, on the other hand, were not as quick to dismiss her wonderings, and her imagination had filled in the details of her friend's appearance, even with no basis to do so. And tonight she had a date with a Domme. She snuggled under the covers, imagining what it might be like to spend a whole evening with someone like one of the heroines of her stories. Would she love it? Or would it be one of those fantasies best left in the imagination?

Worst case scenario, she'd have a great shot at research—could spend the night asking questions and making notes. Wouldn't that be a letdown!

Flicking her gaze toward the clock on the

nightstand, she bolted out of bed for the shower. She was already an hour late for the contest winners' breakfast and would be lucky to arrive downstairs in time for her first panel discussion of the day.

Why hadn't she set the alarm?

# Chapter Two

Mariana pushed her plate away and watched Phil usher the last pair of readers out of the cozy, private dining room the hotel had provided for the winners' breakfast. The made-to-order omelets and waffle stations had been decimated and the fruit and pastry devoured by the twelve women who had shown up. One hadn't….

Her fill-in agent for the weekend returned to her side and pulled out the ever-present tablet.

"Phil, can you get the last goodie bag sent to the reader who didn't make it?" She stood and lifted her sweater from the back of the chair. "You have her snail mail, right?" Assuming the reader hadn't made it to the convention. Perhaps she'd been at the noisy party down the hallway the night before and overslept.

He ran his finger down the screen, nodding. "Sure. Hey, it was Terci Angel. Isn't she the rising-star author who writes those"—he lowered his voice—

"BDSM novels?"

Shock splashed Mariana like icy water even as she suppressed annoyance at his attitude about the genre. How had she missed seeing Terci on the list of attendees? With Mariana's insane travel schedule this year, the events blurred together. She'd known they'd be in the same place at the same time eventually. Even if the other woman didn't know her secret, she'd been hoping for an opportunity to meet her in person, see if she was as delicious as her headshot.

Schooling her features so he wouldn't see how the news affected her, she shrugged. "Yes, I believe she is."

He frowned. "I'm surprised she'd enter your contest. Wasn't it for readers only?"

*Terci.* She pictured the cute blonde with wide, thickly lashed blue eyes and a sprinkling of freckles over her upturned nose. Her image graced the back covers of her books. Books Mariana had helped her write. Or had at least provided research assistance with.

"I'm sorry she didn't make it. I enjoy her work.

She has a unique voice."

He stared at her as if she'd grown another head. "You read her books?"

"Authors are voracious readers, Phil." She would kill Jeanette when she saw her. If she couldn't come herself, fine, but the man rode her last nerve. Perhaps her agent had grasped the opportunity to get him out of her hair while she healed.

"Do you want me to see if Ms. Angel is here? Maybe running late?"

"Phil!" She threw her arms around his neck and squeezed. "You're a genius." Maybe she'd let him live a bit longer. Although a flogging might do him some good. "If she is, see if you can get with her representative and arrange a meet for us. Maybe for a cocktail before dinner. " Despite her protestation, she was also surprised the other author had entered her contest. She would gladly have had breakfast with Terci, or lunch or dinner if she'd asked. Anytime. "And I want to be sure you get that note to my *date* for the evening."

He listened and tapped notes into the tablet. "I will

28

escort you to your next event then go find out if Ms. Angel is in attendance." They strolled out together, and after dropping her off in a conference room, he disappeared.

Things were looking up.

Had there ever been a longer panel?

Terci had arrived at the private dining room for the breakfast to find staff clearing away the buffet and neither a scrap of food nor a single person left from the group who'd gathered to spend time with Mariana Martin. She'd gone to so much trouble to meet her favorite author, but with a full schedule for the day, she'd had to take the time to shower and do her hair and makeup. Darn it.

Her stomach growled as she leaned closer to the microphone to answer a question from a reader about the inspiration for her books. Thank heavens at least coffee had been made available for the panelists. But nothing to eat. How tacky would it be to sneak a bite of granola bar from the emergency rations in her purse?

Very. She'd have to wait a bit longer. What would her dream Mistress have to say about her skipping breakfast? Through poor planning, no less. The meal she'd missed had promised waffles made to order.

The audience shuffled, and she forced herself to focus.

"My research into BDSM?" *Mistress K.*... But she couldn't reveal the name of her benefactor and secret crush. "I have been befriended by several members of the BDSM community," she answered. "They have been unfailingly kind and helpful. Understandably, they would prefer not to be misrepresented in books."

A male gay BDSM author two seats down fielded the next question to the delight of his large group of fans, mostly female, in attendance. Twenty-something, blond and gorgeous, he preened under the attention, and Terci bit her lip to avoid a bitter chuckle. True, these women would never find their way to his bed—his semi-professional football-player boyfriend sat at the back of the room—but how could fantasies hurt? She stood in no position to judge.

Despite her efforts to remain cool and

professional, Terci couldn't shake the dream or the awareness her other crush sat at least fifteen people away, at the far end of the long table. She'd been surprised such a famous author would be on a panel; many preferred not to share the spotlight. Mariana's books—naughty shifters and the humans who love them—were well-suited for the panel on sexy sub-genres. Her presence in a group of others, laughing and charming the crowd with the best of them, added to her appeal. She also took every opportunity to compliment the rest of the panelists, often redirecting questions.

Her voice held the lilt of her birthplace, somewhere in Eastern Europe, although her bio never clarified which part of the former Soviet Union she hailed from. She'd been in the US for most of her adult life...but the exotic hint of faraway places had never left her. Leaning forward, Terci caught a glimpse of the long, dark silky braid trailing over the shoulder of Mariana's sky-blue dress.

Terci planned to make a beeline to the other end of the table the moment the moderator ended the session. At least say hello. Apologize for missing the breakfast. Few authors of Mariana's stature stayed for an entire conference, and she might not have another opportunity. Fishing in her purse, she dug for the schedule. Maybe Mariana and she would be on another panel together. But she'd left the program in her room.

Foot tapping under the table, Terci listened to the moderator thank everyone for attending then gathered her things. As she stood, a group of readers surrounded her, eager to chat. Her heart melted. She couldn't rush out when the opportunity existed to greet those whose support granted her the ability to do the job she loved. Terci signed one book after another, accepting compliments and listening to anecdotes as Mariana sailed out, followed by a thin man in a white button-down shirt and a bow tie, of all things. Her agent? Publicity person?

Maybe she needed to get one of those. Someone to keep her on schedule.

Once again, she scooped up her belongings and started for the door. Mariana was keynote speaker at lunch—one of the reasons for the heavy conference attendance, no doubt. It would be Terci's final opportunity to connect with her idol...so far as she knew.

"Miss Angel?" A young woman with a halo of red curls bouncing around her face, wearing a sunny-yellow print dress and low-heeled pumps, waved a clipboard at her. "I can take you to your table for the luncheon." She lowered her voice. "Do you need to go to the ladies' first?"

Terci blinked. So, when an author achieved a little success...she could no longer go to the bathroom alone? "No, I...." She trailed in the wake of the still-chattering functionary who expressed amazement her agent wasn't present and was "thrilled to meet her," deluging her with questions which she never paused for breath long enough to get answers to.

What a day so far!

# Chapter Three

After another epic failure to connect with Mariana at the luncheon, Terci continued with her workshops and panels, and the day zoomed by without a break. Whenever she got within a hundred feet of her idol, however, someone else claimed her attention. Terci'd fought and struggled and never realized how much even the beginnings of success could take away from her private life. Watching Mariana sail past and into another conference room, accompanied by her small entourage of the bow-tie man and a representative of the conference, Terci worked her way, with the assistance of her new sidekick, Clipboard Girl, through groups who seemed to always block her path and keep her from getting where she needed to be on time.

Brave new world.

By the end of it, she'd shaken hands with several hundred readers, posed for photos with almost as many, and used up so much energy, she sagged in her shoes, unsure she had the strength for her date.

She should have been more aware of what her energy level was likely to be at the end of such a day like this, but what choice did she have?

A little nervous about spending a night learning firsthand about the BDSM lifestyle, she had not wanted to have the encounter at home in case it didn't go well. But when Clipboard Girl—who had apparently been assigned to her for the rest of the event—ushered her into the elevator after dinner and, inserting a key, pressed the P button, Terci'd had enough.

"That's not my floor," she snapped. "And haven't you helped me enough? I am sure I can find my room without any further assistance."

The perky redhead's curls drooped. "I'm sorry, Miss Angel, but the hotel has moved your things to another room."

Terci hit the stop button, and the elevator shuddered to a halt. "They what?" Her voice quivered with outrage and exhaustion.

"A group of readers camped outside your door.

They'd gotten someone to tell them your room number. Just fans, but the fire department doesn't allow blocking of the hallways. The manager decided to move you to a level we can more easily secure."

Terci glanced at the P button on the control panel. "The penthouse?"

"There will be no additional charge, Miss Angel." The doors slid open, and Clipboard Girl stepped out. "It's in the interest of fire safety."

Terci stifled a yawn and followed her to a set of double doors. The assistant slid a keycard, and when the light flashed green, Terci held out her hand. "I can go from here." She'd never been followed around like this before. While it had been convenient in some of the crowds, the woman had gotten between her and readers more than once in the interest of getting her to her next stop, and irritation had lingered at the edges of her mood. Didn't she realize meeting readers was the paramount reason for being here?

Sure, Terci had hoped to meet Mariana, as well, but Clipboard Girl—in the rush and crush her real name had somehow never come up—had been so officious, so insistent she keep moving, she'd never found an opportunity. And, according to the schedule, a copy of which she'd found lying on a table outside the ladies' room, Mariana had no more commitments in the conference, so she'd no doubt made her escape already. Unlike the rest of them, who would be signing the next day Mariana's book signing had been that afternoon and quite an event in itself—but during a time when Terci had other commitments. No, she'd lost her chance to fangirl on her idol. The big ones always had somewhere else to go, places to be, people to see…. They didn't have time to linger like the small fish. And this small fish would probably have made a fool of herself anyway.

"Miss Angel?"

Oh god, her sidekick. "Yes…I'm sorry, I cannot remember your name." She couldn't call her Clipboard Girl aloud, and admitting she'd never asked seemed too rude.

The woman's face crumpled, and she fished in her pocket. "I'm Ivory Flowers. At least, that's my pen name. When the chair learned you didn't have your

37

representative with you, she asked for a committee member to help you out, and I'm such a big fan!"

Terci softened. "Well, it's a pleasure to know your name, Ivory. And thank you for all your help. As an indie author, I don't actually have an agent, you know. I've always made my way around on my own."

Ivory thrust out a book and a Sharpie. "Would you mind terribly signing this for me? I've wanted to ask all day, and, tomorrow, I'll be signing, too. My very first release." She grinned, and a flush crept up her creamy throat to her cheeks, taking her from cute to very sexy. What a shame she wasn't her date...but she didn't look very dominant, and Terci didn't plan to find out if she could swing a flogger herself. At least, not yet. Still, she wouldn't mind a taste of those pink lips, currently tilted in a sweet grin.

"I'd be delighted to sign your book on one condition." The girl's lower lip slipped out in an adorable pout, and Terci stifled a sigh and a smile. "Tomorrow, I will come get one of yours signed."

"Oh, Miss Angel!" Ivory extended the book in trembling hands. "What an honor. My writing group won't even believe me when I tell them…."

"Terci," she admonished. "Now, here"—she took the book, wrote a short note, and signed her name with a flourish—"off you go. I'll find my way around."

"Thank you, Terci. I'll never forget this."

The former Clipboard Girl floated down the hall, clutching the signed volume, and Terci stepped into the suite, shaking her head. The girl's enthusiasm reflected a change in the fans she'd met today. More excited, chirping and giggling at her every word. What a friendly event.

Would her date be able to find her? She quick-typed a note to 1NightStand, giving her changed room number just in case, although she was ready to collapse. With over an hour to relax before her date, she kicked off her high-heeled boots in the foyer and padded through the deep plush of the aqua carpet. The living room sofa and chairs, along with the carpet and draperies, were in shades of blue and sand, almost a beach feel and so serene it calmed her nerves. No matter how wonderful the day—and it had been amazing to meet so many fans and spend time with her fellow authors—the long hours in a crowd, on her best behavior, siphoned her energy and she almost regretted the date.

Couldn't she have worn a wig and gone local? Or asked one of the Dommes over to demonstrate in a more private setting than the public dungeon? Not that she'd feared being seen in the act, but what if it turned out she liked BDSM more in fantasy than practice? In the bedroom, she stopped. If the living room reminded her of the seaside, the bed was an ocean of deep blue, framed in pale wood, hung with curtains billowing to the floor in yards of white. A wave of pillows in blues and teals and lacy-white covered the top third of the mattress. Beautiful, but not where she'd imagined her first time with a Domme might find her.

No, Terci had pictured black and red, and leather and steel. Chains. Swallowing hard, she held her wrists before her, envisioning them bound with rope, smooth and white, and more in tune with the décor. Coils around and around, then looped around a hook on a wall over her head, while Mistress K…no, while her date, whoever she might be, inspected her naked body. The Domme would kick her legs apart and instruct her to keep them there, not move while she donned talons and scraped them over her flesh, raising goose bumps in their wake…*oh god!*

She sought her luggage and found her bag in a closet. Grabbing her shower things and lingerie, she wandered into a bathroom so huge her gasp echoed off the sand-colored tile walls. And the tub…a deep-turquoise porcelain clawfoot in the middle of the room, eclipsing the glass block-enclosed shower along the back wall.

She spun the faucets to send water flowing into the depths and dumped in some foaming milk bath from a silver bowl on a table nearby. Stripping off her clothes and climbing in, she breathed the fragrant steam and considered the other extras available on the stand. A bottle of chilled water sat in a bucket of ice. A plate of fat red strawberries and a bunch of shimmering pale-green grapes. A basket of creams, brushes, and—she swallowed hard again—sex toys also held a piece of paper folded in half. She sank deeper into the warm water, all her muscles relaxing in the soft mounds of bubbles before reaching for the page and opening it.

*To my lovely companion for the evening,*

*I have one simple request....before I enter, don this blindfold and await my pleasure. And yours.*

*Mistress K*

Terci read it again, aloud, but the words didn't change. Mistress K, here, at the hotel. In Canada? Didn't she live in the US somewhere? But she could live in Ottawa or Timbuktu for all the information she'd offered. The woman protected her privacy with vehemence, making it clear from their first conversation that if Terci pushed for personal information, she'd never speak with her again.

Terci had never been so reticent. She'd not only asked questions about the lifestyle, but, during some of their late-night, online chats, she'd shared her own fantasies in great detail. Arching her back, she recalled some of the things she'd told a woman she thought she'd never meet.

And now she'd meet her blindfolded, unable to see her!

A soft click filtered in from the living room, and she shot upright, hands gripping the tub's rounded edges, foam dripping from her shoulders. Another click—the door closing?—and footsteps tapped across the tile foyer. Then a hush. Her heart thudded. Mistress K? Someone from the hotel dropping something off? No, staff would knock first and call to let her know they were there….

It had to be her date.

Terci started to stand, grabbing for the blindfold, but as she still crouched, her foot slipped and she fell back into the water, instinctively holding the black silk strip above the surface.

She lay there a moment, trying to decide whether to sit up and tie the blindfold on or drown and not have to be humiliated rising from the water like a beached whale. Crap on a cracker! The star of her dreams had arrived to make them come true, but

43

could Terci appear like a dignified person? Or even a sexy woman resting on the mound of pillows in her pretty pink satin jammies?

Nope.

Drowning held great appeal. At least until her lungs screamed for air and she emerged gasping and choking to feel someone take the blindfold from her and tie it firmly around her face.

Warm breath blew against her ear. "Stay."

Mariana's heeled boots clicked on the tiles. What an extraordinary situation. Worlds colliding in a grinding crash. It was supposed to be simple, an anonymous date for a little scene. A stranger. Recreation. The handy Phil had not only ensured her note was delivered to her date, but had handed her the key card at dinner so she could let herself into the suite and surprise her anonymous date. Or perhaps not so anonymous.

Instead, a night with a water nymph she knew by name.

Despite her instinctive thrill at a date with Terci

Angel—an amazing chance to offer that home demo…okay hotel demo, big diff—her concern about the danger inherent in the encounter rose. She'd sent a note signed Mistress K. Nobody else would find that odd—but a woman who'd chatted with her late into the night, night after night, would be likely to wonder why she'd set up a date with her blindfolded. True, she'd never let her see her face before, but to meet in person and continue to conceal it?

What a mess. She should turn around and leave, but what excuse could she offer for such rudeness? If she left Terci high and dry—or deliciously wet and slippery—their online friendship would end.

And she'd lose the opportunity of a lifetime. Terci Angel bound and at her mercy. Too sweet to pass up.

Terci's blonde curls dripped with white foam. Bubbles clung to her shoulders and rolled off her perky breasts to reveal dark-rose nipples, the same color as her parted lips. A shame not being able to watch the expression in the sky-blue eyes—one of her favorite "tells" when playing with a sub. But there were other ways to read a sub, and, after all, Mariana had a head start.

Her little online friend had shared so much of herself in their long chats. Would she respond to the fulfillment of her desires? Or would they be things best left to fantasy?

She tightened her grip on the handle of her toy bag then let it fall with a clank. Terci jerked and started to stand.

"No."

She sank back into the tub. Mariana paced around its edge, eyeing the pale, smooth shoulders tapering down toned arms to neatly trimmed nails. She flexed her own hands in approval. Long nails slowed her down on the keyboard. Perhaps Terci had the same issue. While mildly intrigued by acrylics painted with colors and patterns, Mariana found them impractical for so many things. When she wanted the benefit of long nails for scraping along skin, the talons served her well. They would leave nice streaks of pink on the younger author's pale skin.

Or perhaps the vampire gloves?

And what else? Which of Terci's fantasies could

she make come true tonight?

A whimper from the water drew her attention.

"Have you finished bathing?"

Terci extended an arm covered with goose bumps. "The water is chilling, Mistress. May I get out?"

"So well-behaved," she crooned, tracing a finger over a wet forearm. "I wonder if you will be so good when we begin to play. You want to play, don't you?"

Terci nodded, damp curls bobbing. "Yes, Mistress, so much."

"You know who I am?" Mariana grasped her palm and helped her to her feet.

"Yes." Stepping out of the tub, Terci wobbled. To move with grace while blindfolded, or even staying upright, took practice. She regained her balance and sighed. "You are Mistress K, my online friend."

"I am glad to meet you in person. But just as you never saw me during our conversations, you may not see me tonight." Mariana reached for a fluffy white towel and patted the other woman dry, brushing aside lingering bubbles on her torso. For their one night, her identity must be protected. They weren't starting a relationship. "If you wish to continue, I must have your word you will leave the blindfold in place, no matter what."

# Chapter Four

*No matter what....*

Terci shuddered as Mistress K dabbed the towel over her throat and down her back in smooth strokes. Curiosity held her in its sway, but curiosity about what? She'd set the whole evening up for the purpose of filling the gaps in her knowledge of BDSM with real-world experience.

But how many late nights had she curled up in bed, the laptop propped on a pillow beside her, sharing her deepest desires with a woman she'd never seen? Did she resemble the dream Mistress? Her power and compassion came across even in typed instant messages, but her appearance remained a mystery.

Warm lips brushed her jaw. "You may not see me, but you can have everything else."

*Ohhh.* "I won't peek. But I am not...not sure I really can do...or have you do...everything we talked about. I mean, it sounded exciting, but what if I change my mind? Get scared? Want out?"

A sharp slap to her butt sent her stumbling forward before Mistress K steadied her again. "After all our lessons, you have to ask what to do if you want play to slow? Or stop?" A hand circled Terci's arm, but another crack against her bath-warmed skin threatened to buckle her knees. "Tell me your safeword."

"I don't—" *Crack!* "Ouch, that hurt!"

"Good. Don't make me wait. Safeword." The body heat that was Mistress K disappeared and Terci stood alone, blindfolded, with panic edging in. Then her wrist was clasped and yanked behind her back. "Link your fingers and keep them there until I tell you to release them."

"My safeword is popcorn, candy corn if I want to slow down." She shivered, naked skin cooling in the air. "Is that okay?"

"It's your word. Whatever you choose." The voice moved farther away, and Terci turned her head right and left, as if it would enable her to see. "Come here."

Shuffling one foot then the other, she made her

way in the direction of Mistress K's voice. With her arms behind her back, she couldn't reach out, feel for the doorway, the walls, the tub. She was so turned around and more than a little afraid she'd stumble again. "Marco."

Mistress K choked. Laughing? "I am not about to respond Polo."

"I lost my sense of direction."

"You're facing me. Continue forward, and you will be at the bed in ten steps."

Terci pushed her feet forward, counting, *one, two, three*....at *ten*, her toe bumped against something solid, and her arms twitched with the need to come around and break her fall, her fingers tightening their grip on one another against every instinct as she plummeted down, down, and landed with a bounce on the mattress. She slid off the slippery coverlet to kneel on the floor at the side of the bed.

When she scrambled to get to her feet, a hand on her shoulder held her in place. "I like you there for the moment, kneeling at my feet. I am seated to your right. And we have negotiations to complete before I lay a finger on you."

"But you just did!"

Mistress K twisted her fingers in her hair and gave a tug. "A loving spank, something any vanilla couple would do. I want to discuss the things you dreamed of."

Dreamed.... She'd never shared her actual dreams, had she? The ones about the dungeon? Trying to remember, she bit her lip. "Okay." It seemed much easier in her books to negotiate hard and soft limits. Kneeling naked at her Mistress's side, she couldn't think what to do, what to say. "I need you to help me."

A low chuckle accompanied the sweep of fingers across her cheekbone. "That's what I'm here for."

"You are?"

"Maybe. But we have to start somewhere. We spoke of many things, you and I, and the only hard limits you thought you'd have were...?"

"Knives, needles, and blood play."

"Soft limits?

"Anal play and strap-ons."

"There are so many possibilities, but in one night, your first time, I won't be bringing out the big guns. So, we can begin. On your feet, my Terci."

Her heart thudded. *My Terci.* Sweet mother! How had she ever had the guts to ask this woman questions? Distance helped. In person, she seemed bigger than life, even without the ability to see her. Awkward without her hands to help, Terci clambered to her feet and stood with her knees touching the edge of the mattress, giving her some idea of where she stood in space. The idea calmed her.

"Shoulders back, thrust out those tits."

She complied, breasts lifting as she arched, deep pink nipples an offering Mariana accepted. Cupping the underside of one breast, she lifted it and pressed the flat of her tongue to the tightened peak. A shudder ran through Terci, and she steadied her.

"Nice, feet apart"—she shoved them wider with her boot—"and keep them like that."

Mariana licked around the nipple, enjoying the texture and the trace of salt from perspiration already breaking out on the clean skin. Moving to the other side, she drew the tautness into her mouth and bit down just enough to elicit a squeak.

"Do you like that, Terci? You never mentioned biting when we spoke late at night, but if you are a very good girl, and ask nicely, I might be persuaded to leave some teeth marks on this lovely skin."

"Yes, Mistress." Terci's stance helped keep her upright, but if she trembled any more, she'd be in a heap at Mariana's feet. Not a bad thing, she mused, tracing circles around one nipple then the other, enjoying the shivers of her new sub.

"I brought my toys with me, sweet. I can show you all the things you asked about."

Terci panted. "So you knew it would be me? Did you ask for me?"

Mariana stepped back and took in the room, considering where to begin. "No," she said. "This date was a gift from a friend. I didn't know about it until today." As the other woman's shoulders drooped, she moved in again and pinched her cheek. "But I would have asked if I'd known you were an option."

More than asked. Demanded. Her online friend's skin glowed in the lamplight, the freckles dusting her nose also creating a haze over her collarbone and the top of her chest. But, from there, it was all smooth, pale softness and rosy nipples.

Clasping Terci's arm, she turned her to face the bed. "What a tasty morsel you are." Skating her hand from shoulder past her nipped-in waist and bringing it to rest on the flare of her hip, she paused. "Tell me, all those nights we talked, those questions you asked...did you hope I'd help you fulfill your fantasies one day?"

"You were kind enough to help me be accurate. I wanted to please the readers."

"I saw your readers flocking around you today. They love you." Accurate and passionate both...nobody could write a BDSM story so effectively if she didn't feel it, at least a little. "But you didn't answer me, and I think for that you must be punished." She gave her a little push, and Terci fell forward onto the ocean of a bed, her skin like pure cream among the blues and greens of the comforter and pillows. "This is one night only, and I don't want to waste a moment."

"No, Mistress," she said, turning her face to the side, and the words became less muffled. "I mean, I don't want to waste any time, either."

" Safeword?"

"Popcorn."

"Wait for me."

Mariana took her time retrieving her toy bag, knowing the delay would enhance the other woman's anticipation, arousal. Why she brought it to every conference, she had no idea. She'd never used it at one, keeping her personalities separate. She'd considered slipping away to local dungeons as Mistress K, but so many others in the book world were active in the lifestyle, and if another attendee showed up and realized the connection, her privacy would be over.

Silly to hide her active lifestyle side probably, but she'd never found the right time to step out of her shell. A few of her shifter characters dabbled in

BDSM, but she'd yet to jump into the genre, unlike the intrepid Terci.

Returning to her side, Mariana dropped the bag with a clank again, enjoying the woman's jump. "I'm back." Fishing out a pair of leather, lambskin-lined cuffs, she dragged them down Terci's back, allowing the buckles to redden the skin in their path. "Did you miss me?"

"Y-yes, Mistress."

"Roll over and bring your hands to the front." Mariana fastened each cuff on a wrist and grasped Terci's elbow, tugging her to her feet. "Arms above your head." Tossing a length of silken rope over the top of the bedframe, she threaded the ends through the cuffs and shortened the length until the other woman rose onto her tiptoes. "Are you comfortable?"

"Not really."

"Excellent." The bag yielded a soft suede flogger. "I have more questions to ask you, but since you had trouble answering the first one, and have already earned punishment, I thought we might as well have you in the right position as we go." She let the tails fall onto Terci's back. No impact. Just letting her know what was there.

Terci shuddered. "Yes, Mistress."

Caressing her with the toy, Mariana trailed the flogger down to the floor and gave a sharp snap at her ankles. "Legs apart. Always, unless I tell you different."

"Yes, Mistress."

How cooperative. Terci'd always been sweet and curious in their chats, but in person she seemed too cooperative. Was she frightened? Terci had shared that no man or woman had ever taken her beyond the vanilla, and the reality often held more of a challenge for a newbie. Mariana would watch her reactions, avoid taking her somewhere she might not want to go, exercise care with her own desires. Domspace could make perfect control difficult to achieve.

"As I recall"—Mariana continued to toy with her, bringing the flogger up along the inside of her calves, her thighs and then stopping short of the prize—"we often spoke of flogging and other impact play, for punishment or pleasure. You even thought of taking a class at your local dungeon, didn't you?" Mightn't that have been interesting if she had.

"Yes, Mistress." The muscles in Terci's back flinched as Mariana again brushed the soft suede there. "But I didn't want to go to a class on my own."

"Ah, I see. So you couldn't take your professional curiosity into the real world. What were you afraid of? You might not like what you learned?"

"No," Terci murmured, so low she had to strain to hear.

"Then what?" Drawing back the flogger, Mariana gave a sharp snap and reddened a swath across the delicious buttocks she wanted to bite. How lucky the woman would allow nibbling. And how odd it hadn't come up in their chats.

Terci jumped again and settled back on her toes, the long line of her legs and body a perfect image, her curves keeping her from looking too lean. Feminine perfection. "That I might like it too much."

"Really. So maybe, now, you have an answer for my earlier question. Everything you talked about, did you imagine us together acting them out? A little scene?" Another flick and another, a flurry reddening the soft skin on her sit spot.

"Is there something wrong with me?" She arched away from the flogger's continuing stripes, but with her hands so high above her head, she had nowhere to go. "I never got enough out of sex, not like all my friends talked about. And I met you and then...I wondered if maybe I needed pain for happiness."

Mariana tossed the toy toward the bag and gathered Terci against her, reaching around to grasp her breasts and pinch the nipples between thumb and forefinger. "Like this? You were afraid you'd be turned on if someone pinched your nipples, twisted them, pulled on them like this?"

"Yes!"

"You wanted to please your readers." One hand stroked down, palm flat on her belly, gliding past the groomed strip of blonde hair and cupping her mound. "But did you want to please yourself? To please a Mistress?" The silky evidence of Terci's arousal coated her fingers. She lowered her voice. "To please me?"

The perfume of her cream rose, and Mariana breathed it in. Clean woman, her favorite fragrance. Terci had a relationship history peppered with men and women, but Mariana didn't do sex with men. She would top them on occasion. But the act didn't hold the piquancy of an armful of willing woman.

"To please you," she said. "I dreamed of pleasing you. Every night."

Mariana had told herself lust sometimes happened when people talked about passion in all its many hues night after night. She responded to the eagerness of a person who wanted to know all about the lifestyle and who wrote it with such a deft hand. But her Terci had dreamed of her, every night....

"And when you dreamed of me, did you wake up as wet as this?" Gliding a finger into the slick channel, she asked, "Did you touch yourself?" She added a second and nuzzled the side of Terci's neck, sucking on the softest skin she'd ever touched, tasted. "Did you come thinking of me?"

A long silence, and Mariana kept fingering her, but removed the other hand from her breast and slapped her flank. Hard.

"Answer me. And be truthful, or I will know." She waited but no answer came. "Face me."

Twisting in her bonds, Terci turned on tiptoe. Two fat tears trailed down her cheeks below the blindfold. "I'm ashamed."

Mariana grasped two handfuls of her curls and dragged her closer. She kissed her forehead, her cheeks, her nose and finally her lips. Softly, offering compassion. "Never be ashamed of pleasure. I am glad you would think of me and reach orgasm." Her grip in Terci's hair tightened, dragging her head back to bare her throat. "But from now on, you will ask permission." Burying her face in the fragrant skin, she sucked a mouthful in and bit down, marking her. "I won't have you using me for your pleasure unless I give leave."

"But, this is only for one night." Terci swallowed hard, writhing in Mariana's grip. "What about after this?"

"Terci, we are already friends. If you are aroused by an online conversation, a phone call, or my mouth on your clit, you may not come without my permission and—maybe—my assistance."

"Even after tonight?" Her voice broke, but Mariana didn't attend anyone's pity party.

She jerked on her hair again. "Tonight is special. Let's enjoy it and then worry about the rest of our lives." Eyeing the bruise forming on the pale skin of Terci's neck, Mariana drew in a calming breath. "So…it is true, isn't it? After we talk, you dream, and after you dream, you touch yourself."

"Not always."

# Chapter Five

*Not* always? *How pathetic am I? She's going to walk away and leave me hanging here until someone from Housekeeping comes tomorrow.* Terci flexed her fingers, wincing at the pins and needles shooting through them. She wouldn't really leave her, would she?

Mistress K barked out a laugh and released her hair. "You mean you only get yourself off sometimes after we talk? I should charge you for my services, but I'm not that kind of a Dominant."

"I'm sorry, Mistress." As if she could apologize for such a thing. Sure, people had cybersex, but she never had considered asking Mistress K to engage in it with her. She'd have died first. "It's just, all the things we talk about stay in my mind." Vibrators, bondage, cold steel against warm flesh...fire....

Mistress K loosened the rope, her fingers working the knots, brushing Terci's. Lowering her arms halfway, she gasped at the shooting pains of returning circulation.

"You'll get used to it. With a little practice, you will build tolerance."

She rubbed her elbows. "I don't think one night is going to be enough to build tolerance."

"There is no reason you cannot play after you return home, is there? We both know you like it."

Terci had never felt so alive, but she couldn't do things like this with a stranger. "It's different with you. I'm still not sure I'd trust someone else like this."

"You didn't know it would be me tonight, and you were prepared to allow a stranger to tie you up and do all sorts of naughty things to you."

Damn her for her logic.

"Madame Eve's service comes highly recommended. At the very least, I felt confident I wouldn't be killed or severely damaged." Terci sank onto the bed with a sigh. "But you have a point. If it hadn't been you, I am not sure if I'd have had the courage to go through with it. I'm not very brave."

"You're brave." Mistress K sat next to her and

bumped her shoulder. "You talked to me online about the most intimate details of your life. You gave up a successful career, on the way to a corner office, to take the jump into publishing. You have the courage of your convictions."

"Well, I hated my job, so I'm not sure it reflects all that well on me to leave something I hated to do something I love."

"I think that may be the very definition of bravery." The mattress moved as Mistress's weight lifted, and fabric rustled for a moment before the Domme rejoined her.

*Is she naked?* Terci's wrists were still cuffed, but they weren't linked, so she had full use of her hands. If she stretched one out, what would she find?

"Can I take the blindfold off now?" She reached toward her face, but Mistress K caught her hand and held it. "Please?"

"Not yet, my Terci," Mistress K said. "You may be brave, but I have spent years protecting my identity. I think I will continue a bit longer."

"We've known each other for such a long time,

months, over a year?"

"Yes."

"And in all that time I haven't been able to put a face to the words. Can I ask you anything about yourself?"

"No."

"But you know all about me." She pouted. "This isn't fair."

Mariana's laugh rang out. "Nobody said anything was fair. This is BDSM and I, my dear, am a sadist. Torturing you is my great pleasure."

Terci flopped onto her back, legs dangling off the edge of the bed. "This is so frustrating! I've wanted to see you, meet you since we've known one another. You really are cruel."

"Sadists often are."

"Well, crap on a cracker!"

"That will cost you." Mariana grabbed her arm and positioned her over her lap, head hanging down, fingers braced on the floor. A warm hand stroked circles on her, slow and soothing where the flogger had already stung. "I see a few stripes, but this fanny is too smooth and unbruised for my liking. Reach into the bag on the floor to the right of your hands. I'll need a hairbrush for this."

And probably not to arrange her hair.

"What are you going to do with it?"

"No speaking without permission." The soothing stopped and an openhanded spank drove heat through Terci's extremities. "Do you want me to have to ask you twice to get the brush?"

Terci patted the floor and found the duffel unzipped. Fishing inside, she located the bristly wooden implement and pulled it out. "No. Here it is."

"And my talon case, in the outer pocket."

*Ohhh.* Talons had sounded so sexy. They'd been an amazing addition to her second book, *My Dom's sub.* And one of her favorite fantasies. But....

"You aren't going to spank me with talons?"

"Not anymore." Another sharp smack. "Now, I want the vampire gloves."

Terci reached into the outer pocket. "No, I have the talons. See?" She held them over her shoulder, showing her cooperation. "No need for vampire gloves."

Unlike the talons, which headed her wish list, she actually owned a pair of the gloves, purchased to be examined as a device in the next book. She'd worn them for a while, getting a feel for them. Each finger held dozens of steel tacks which, when she'd run them down her arm, stung like tiny bees.

Mistress K took them from her uplifted hand. "Get the gloves, too. We'll see how you behave during your spanking and decide which I want to play with. I enjoy both."

Would it be so enjoyable on the receiving end? Terci rummaged around in the depths of what felt like a canvas duffel and finally came across butter-soft leather with sharp pins embedded in the fingers and, with a mental wince, passed them to the Domme.

"Good girl. But next time I expect you to follow my orders more quickly."

"Yes, Mistress."

"Why are you being punished?"

She didn't remember… panic and lust flooded her brain with adrenalin and she barely remembered her own name—the real one or the pen name. Why…why? "Because I didn't answer your question. And because I didn't obey you fast enough."

"Yes." A warm palm, friendly and soothing, rubbed her behind again. "And?"

And? "Because I said crap on a cracker?"

"Exactly."

"Do you have a problem with cursing?"

"No…just repulsive images."

Would she have her skin scored by slaps with a vampire glove? An arm came down on her waist and a leg pinned her thighs before the wooden back repeatedly peppered her backside. Mistress K worked from the top of the mounds, to the sit spot to the crease, to her thighs, and back again while heat and pain rose. Terci's clit throbbed in rhythm and a trickle of moisture traced through her slit.

Hell, maybe the vampire gloves were a good idea if a hairbrush turned her on this much. She wanted to touch herself but couldn't think how to balance without her fingers braced on the floor and also couldn't think how to sneak them between Mistress

K's lap and her own body. If she didn't get some more direct contact to her pussy soon, she'd come anyway.

Impact play. Been there done that, wanted the T-shirt.

"There!" Mistress K helped her sit up and cuddled her on her lap. "All is forgiven."

Terci's behind pulsed as she sat on the Domme's naked thighs. According to her research, many times the top stayed clothed, but there were no rules—at least not for tops. "Thank you, Mistress."

"You're welcome, Terci. You have pleased me with your acceptance of your punishment. Have you been spanked before?"

"Never, not even as a child." She tried not to think too much about her burning bottom or her aching pussy. "My parents believed 'use the rod and ruin the child.'"

"I am not a believer in spanking children either." She pinched Terci's side. "But a sexy, grown-up woman…big fan. If only you could see how rosy your skin looks after the hairbrush."

"I could without the blindfold."

"I beg your pardon?"

"Nothing, Mistress." She wriggled a little, trying to find a non-painful part of her backside, with little effect. "Nothing important." Terci's head rested against the lean torso, but the Domme's bare breasts were soft and pillowy.

"Now, Terci, we can get back to what we were talking about before I needed to pause for punishment time."

Despite her promise, Terci tilted her head this way and that, hoping for a glimpse of the Mistress. But the black silk kept her blind to everything except the occasional bit of light at the edges. "I await your pleasure."

"A line from your most recent book."

"A line from my heart." The words spilled from her lips. But they were true. She'd put them in the story with this Domme in mind. It had been Mistress K's hands she'd pictured bringing pain and pleasure to the heroine.... But nothing could have prepared her for how her online crush would bloom into something so much more—still sight unseen.

Her voice, her warm skin, her very touch lit fires Terci'd never known could burn. She wanted to explore the woman's body, learn every inch of it, and please her, to fall at her feet and worship her for her strength, her kindness, and how wonderful she smelled. Like the ocean with a tropical breeze.

"Mistress?" She'd gotten all sloppy sentimental, even if most of it had been in her head.

"Show me."

She flicked her gaze left to right, behind their covering, as if the explanation could be found there. "Show you what…Mistress?" Naked already, she had bared her feelings. What more could she show?

"Crawl to the head of the bed and show me how you pleasure yourself after you've dreamed of me."

*She can't mean it.*

"But I can't…."

Warm breath brushed her ear. "Do you want to spend more of our precious time on punishment for disobedience?"

Why pretend she didn't want to play? Her body

ached with suppressed need. She'd move through any discomfort for release. And to show her Mistress how far she would go to be worthy of her. "Can you give me a start in the right direction?"

What a delight! The subbie to end all subs—if only she had more than one night with Terci, more time to spend together. But if they met again, she'd have to show herself—bring the fragmented parts of her persona together or swear Terci to secrecy.

A burden she didn't wish on another. And Terci's books were starting to climb the charts. She wouldn't have time to worry about another's secrets as she reached success. Mariana might have helped her with some details, but the talent was all her own.

She'd heard three agents fighting over her in the foyer. At dinner, a representative of one of the biggest publishers in New York had approached Terci, but she hadn't even acted excited. Her sales were soaring, and she seemed to have no idea she'd gone from an up-and-coming author to one who had arrived—the indie sensation of the year.

No…one night would have to be enough, at least for now.

Pushing back the thoughts threatening to drown her, Mariana turned her attention back to the hours remaining in their single night. She'd take it all the way to dawn, enjoy every moment, and make memories to last as long as possible.

The sight of Terci propped against the pillows set her on fire. The sub lifted a hand and held it in the air as if uncertain what to do.

"Don't stop…I want to see."

Cupping her hand over her mound, Terci dipped the tips of her fingers between her legs but paused again.

"Do I have to tie your legs apart before you will share with me what you do *with me* in your thoughts?"

*Is that a nod?*

Cheeky girl!

"Never dare me—" With a regretful glance at the intricately-carved bedposts, she picked up the silken rope and fetched another piece and ankle cuffs from the bag. She'd prefer to use steel. Handcuffs, chains…all the things she loved best and Terci had sounded so interested in.

In her own fantasies, her own dreams, chains always played a role. Terci in chains.

Still, she grasped one of Terci's ankles, buckled on the cuff then tied it to the bedpost, repeating the action on the other side, spreading her wide. The rope would not damage the wood, but served to immobilize the smooth legs. Mariana knelt on the foot of the bed.

"So exposed," she purred. "Try again. And if you don't show me how you really do it, I'll know, and I won't let you come all night."

Terci's horrified expression was comical—but Mariana suppressed her laughter. Which became easier when the other woman gave a long stroke from front to back. God, could she be any sexier? Lounging against the pillows, with her golden curls making a halo around her face, her cheeks and throat flushed with passion. Her chest rose and fell as she rubbed herself, circling her clit, stroking again….

"What are you thinking of, my Terci?" Mariana crept closer, halfway up the bed, stopping between the sub's knees. "Are you thinking of me?"

"Only of you, Mistress. Of your hands, your lips, the tip of your flogger." She rubbed faster, panting. "Of the little vibrator you told me about, the one with the clit stimulator and…and—"

Mariana clasped her wrist, stilling her movements. "You aren't thinking of coming without permission, are you?"

"No," she muttered, hips bucking against their joined hands. "Can I have permission?"

It got hard to keep control when up against the sexiest thing on two legs, a sub with the ability to make her laugh.

"Do you think you should come before I do?" Mariana asked, steadying her voice.

Terci's face fell. "No, Mistress."

Mariana wrapped her arms around the other woman's hips. "Then it's lucky for you I am in charge." Bending her neck she buried her face in the sweetness of Terci's pussy. She lapped at her cream like a hungry cat and drew her clit into her mouth to suck and toy with. A low growl escaped. What was this woman doing to her?

Terci's hands buried in her hair, tangled in the braid falling down her back. "Please, please, please," she chanted.

Mariana lifted her face. "Come, Terci. I want my turn as well.

With a gasp, the sub bucked against her, and Mariana tightened her grip to hold her steady, sucking steadily on her clit, tickling the tip with her tongue. Juices flowed down Mariana's chin as Terci sobbed out her pleasure and begged her to stop, don't stop...and stop again.

When she fell limp, Mariana did stop, resting her forehead on Terci's stomach for a moment, then rolled to the floor to get some things from her bag. Sometimes she amazed herself with the number of interesting items she managed to carry in it. She never knew what would suit the moment until she got there and was enough of a Girl Scout to never want to be unprepared.

Returning to kneel between Terci's legs, she admired the flushed pussy still shiny with cream. The work of a moment to insert the vibrator and position the clit stimulator where it would do the most good. "I hope you don't think we're done for the night. I have so many more plans for our time together."

Terci nodded sleepily, but when Mariana pushed the button for low speed on the remote, she squealed. "Is that what I think it is?"

"The vibrator I told you about. Isn't it everything I said it would be?"

"I'm not ready yet." She squirmed. "I need some recovery time."

"What are you," Mariana asked, scooting back to the foot of the bed, "a man?" The vampire gloves lay by one of Terci's feet, and Mariana drew them on. "I'm sure we can get you back in the mood."

Terci wriggled as if trying to escape and muttered something under her breath.

"Enough." Mariana took another length of rope and tied Terci's cuffed wrists to the top posters of the bed and sighed. "It's my turn." Straddling her face, she drew one glove along the sub's side, the tacks leaving pale red streaks. "No biting now...that's my job.

Mariana gasped at the first touch of Terci's tongue on her pussy and lowered herself so the sub could reach her better. Warm lips, tongue, and mouth worked her pussy with expertise. She might be new at BDSM, but this wasn't Terci's first time eating out another woman. A stab of jealousy at the thought pulled her out of the moment for a second. What right did she have to worry about who else Terci experienced pleasure with? It wasn't as if she'd collared her.

While she still had some sense of reality, Mariana put the gloves to use, gliding them over Terci's skin with a delicate touch. She didn't want to break the skin and cross the line Terci had set. No blood. The gloves offered intense sensory play. Goose bumps followed her hand as she covered every inch of torso then, when Terci drew her clit into her mouth and sucked, she pulled off the gloves and removed the vibrator, burying her own face in the warm sweetness again, not stopping until they both shook with powerful release.

# Chapter Six

The sound of an old-fashioned phone ringing startled Terci awake. She stared into the early morning shadows and tried to put together what had happened the night before. So many dreams ended this way. Her alone in bed after a night of being subject to Mistress K and her many devious and painful pleasures. She rolled onto her back and stifled a cry.

Feeling her backside with delicate fingers, she traced a series of even welts across her bottom. It had been no dream. She'd spent a night with Mistress K. She'd either taken research to a new level or truly crossed over into the dark side. As the rising sun sent more light into the room, the furnishings came into view. Not a dungeon, the suite had served its purpose as one. Unlike the dungeon of her dreams, it was neither underground nor dark, and its light and airy appearance gave no clue to the activities of the night before.

The pillow next to her held a dent from her Mistress's head, but a long, dark hair remained. Dark brown. A visual clue to Mistress K's appearance. She closed her eyes again and tried to put together an image. Slim and toned, with soft, uptilted breasts and narrow hips.

Her hair braided, or it had been until Terci had managed to unweave the strands at some point during the night to bury her face in the waterfall of scented silk. She smelled like the ocean. And she had a ring on her second toe—discovered when Terci had been granted the privilege of worshiping the Domme's body with her lips—a pleasure she'd stretched out as long as possible. *Ohhh*. She gave a delicate shiver at the memory, her nipples hardening.

But the Mistress still seemed absolutely determined to protect her identity.

Why?

And what brought her here? Was she Canadian? Or…did she have another reason to be in Ottawa this weekend?

The phone rang again, and Terci stood, groaning.

Not her ringtone, maybe the hotel phone. But no...it came from under the bed. She got down on her knees and reached as far under as she could, withdrawing an android phone. Should she answer it? It might well have fallen out of a housekeeper's pocket while making the bed. Or could it be...she pushed the answer button and hoped the caller would give her a clue.

"Mariana? It's Phil."

*Mariana?* The phone slipped from her fingers. The electronic sound of a voice at a distance continued until she picked it up again.

"Phil? This is Terci Angel."

Silence.

"Phil, Mariana left her phone in my room by mistake last night. Could you ask her to come pick it up sometime in the next hour or two?"

"Oh, I can come get it. What room are you in?"

"No," she said. "I would like to personally give it to her."

"Umm, sure, if I can track her down. She might be anywhere in the hotel. If you see her first, would you tell her I'm looking for her?" His voice rose in pitch. "My sister will kill me if I make her late for her meeting with her publisher."

She shrugged aside the random blatherings, too consumed with her own thoughts to worry about who his sister might be or why she might want to kill him. "Sure will." She tapped the phone for a second. "And tell her I've taken off the blindfold and know the truth."

The man's voice seemed skeptical. "And will she know what that means?"

"Yes, I think so." Terci disconnected and went into shower. Her thoughts swirled more than the water going down the drain.

Mariana Martin, one of the top three romance authors in North America, maybe the world... Mistress K? Sure, Mariana wrote sexy shifters, but a Domme? And all the time, Terci had been picking her brain for her own books...she'd been talking to Mariana?

Impossible. Mariana wasn't a BDSM writer—at least not for the most part.

But if not her, what was the truth? She stepped under the steaming spray and shivered even in the heat. She felt like she'd been with two women the night before.

Mistress K, who she knew from the Internet and had had a crush on for months.

And Mariana Martin, the author who everyone knew and whose books Terci devoured the moment they were released.

Which one had she slept with—not that they'd slept much.

Or both?

She'd spent the day before trying to meet her favorite author without success.

Had she then slept with her?

Too much to take in. Shampooing her hair, she pictured the back cover image from one of Mariana's books. Her long, silky braid, aqua eyes, and thick lashes. Cupid's bow mouth. She compared it to the image she'd put together of Mistress K based on other senses.

Since she'd had her vision hampered, she'd been

limited to what she'd been able to touch, hear, and smell. And taste. Hard to compare the two women. But it had to be her, or how else could her phone have wound up under the bed?

She finished showering and wrapped one voluminous towel around her hair, another around her body. The array of bath and body products didn't tempt as it had earlier. She was too caught up in her thoughts. The wonder.

Had she spent the night with her date, her mentor, and her favorite author…and a Domme all rolled into one? Like having ice cream, cake, pie, cookies, and a Lindt truffle all in the same perfect bite?

As she moved back into the bedroom, she heard a rap at the door. "Who is it?"

"Me."

Still hiding her identity? Still? So she didn't ask who she meant or bother to dress. Just strolled over to the door and pulled it open.

"Hello, Mariana…Mistress K…or whoever you are." What else was there to say? The woman had kept her tied up, tied down, and everything in between for an entire night. She'd given her more orgasms than she'd known she could receive. And she'd stolen her heart. How could she not have given her heart to someone who gave so much to her? "Let me get your phone."

Mariana wore another blue dress, enhancing her eyes. The eyes Terci hadn't been able to see while they'd made love for hours on end. The towel wrapped around her own torso seemed less than appropriate for their meeting, but she wouldn't leave to put on something else.

"Terci, can I come in? I can explain."

"No, you probably can't explain all this away, but come in anyway. No point having this conversation in the hallway." She stepped aside, and Mariana strolled in. Despite her anger, Terci had no desire to cause Mariana any professional problems.

Following the other author, she paused long enough to admire the sway of her hips under the shirt dress. Maybe she'd erred and the phone had gotten into the room some other way? A housekeeper had stolen her phone or—more likely—found it and tucked it in a pocket then lost it. No way had she had sex on every surface but the ceiling with Mariana Martin and not even known it.

The slender body implied otherwise. And the long, dark hair, back in its silky braid.

Terci closed the door to the hallway and turned to face the living room.

Mariana shifted uneasily, showing none of the aplomb Terci would expect from a bestselling author and Domme. "Was it the phone, or did you figure it out during the night?

Terci shrugged. "You know when I have those dreams? The Mistress in the dreams. She was you. I thought I imagined Mistress K, but I never had an idea of what she...you looked like, so my subconscious used...your appearance. I guess my subconscious had it right. Even if I didn't know it." She blinked back a few stray tears. "Tell me, Mariana, how long were you going to let me wonder? Or could you really walk away without an explanation?"

The other woman parted her lips, but snapped

them closed again.

"You don't have an explanation."

"No. How did you figure it out? I took off the blindfold before I left. I didn't want you to be frightened if you woke with it on, but you were asleep."

"The phone clued me in. Until it rang and I found it under the bed, right near where your bag had been, I had no idea. Are you Canadian?" What about her Eastern European accent?

"No, not at all," Mariana interjected helpfully.

"But do you live in Canada?" Seems like her back-cover bio called her an American author...as in US. Born in Eastern Europe.

"No." Terci fought back irritation. Even as she began to share, Mist—Mariana still held back. Not Canadian. A pittance of information.

"I started to figure out Mistress K had to be someone at the convention, an author or at least someone in the business...but how could it be you? I'm in your fan club. And now you've seen me naked."

Mariana gaped for a second then burst into laughter and linked their hands together. "I've seen you bound, naked, and with your face between my legs. I hardly think the naked part is the most interesting, although I did enjoy it." She led Terci toward the sofa where she sat and drew her down beside her. "It's hard to be open. Only my agent knows about my alternate persona."

"That guy who followed you around all day? With the bow tie?"

"Okay, my agent, her fiancée, and, as of this weekend, I suppose Phil does, too. At least he knows about the name 'Mistress K,' from the note he delivered."

"I guess it's coming-out day." Terci fought the urge to lean closer to Mariana, needing a bit of distance to keep her thoughts straight. "And you were prepared to walk away...without ever letting me see your face, know who you were?"

"I tried to...but I couldn't." Mariana tugged her closer. "I had to come back. Terci, it's time I stopped hiding who I am, but you have a career just starting and I don't know if there will be backlash or what readers will think if I come out as who I really am."

Terci pulled back. "Why would readers have a problem with you? And why would I care if they had one with me? I hope they love my work, but I don't think I need to present my life on a platter. And I've never been asked to. Why are you so worried about it?"

Mariana's lips tilted in a soft smile that lit even her eyes. "Maybe I'm not anymore. Maybe it's time I brought all my life parts together."

She searched the Domme's face for any stress. How had such a thing held them apart for so long? "Or maybe it's not. But it doesn't matter. How you live your life is your business. Can I see you again?"

Mariana cupped her chin and pressed her lips to Terci's forehead then her cheek and spoke against her mouth. "Yes." Her kiss held promise for the future, and Terci drank deep of its sweetness until they stopped to breathe. She snuggled closer, though, needing the contact to assure her they were truly together.

"I'd come to your home"—Terci petted the soft fabric of the blue dress covering a body she wanted to see—"but I don't even know where you live."

"I live about fifteen miles from you."

She jumped to her feet. "What? All this time you've been in the next town over? Why...I might have seen you at the store. But I didn't because I would have noticed Mariana Martin even if I didn't know you were also my friend, Mistress K." She sank onto the floor by the Domme's knees and rested her head there, her throat thick with emotion. "I wish I'd seen you."

"No, I never saw you either," Mariana said, toying with Terci's curls. "But I did suggest you go to the dungeon."

Was she a member? "Yes, we talked about my taking classes. Flogging classes."

Mariana's chuckle sent warmth through Terci's body, centering in her pussy. "I teach flogging there. I thought if you saw me there, if you knew me there, in my leathers and boots, you'd accept me as Mistress K and not realize I am Mariana. At least until we could spend some time together. But you never came to class. And the time you did come to visit, I didn't know until you told me afterward."

She blew out a breath. "I wish I'd signed up for your class."

"Me, too."

Silence descended, comfortable, while Terci melted under the Domme's touch on her hair. Did a sub suggest the Domme make love to her? Was there a proper way to do that?

"Will you take my class when we get home? This week?"

"Looking for someone to demonstrate on?"

Mariana's fingers tightened in her hair. "Feeling brave, are we? I have half a mind to drag you into the cavernous bedroom and put you over my lap."

"Mistress, I'll come on a leash, with a hairbrush held between my teeth, if it means I can be with you."

# ~A Note from Kate~

Thank you for buying the latest in the *In Chains* subseries, part of the award winning 1Night Stand Series from Decadent Publishing. I give most of the credit for accuracy to the men and women in the BDSM community who have kindly shared their experiences over the past few years, especially the Doms and Dommes of The Lair, San Antonio who share Mistress K's hopes for understanding and accurate representation of their lifestyle.

As for me...I believe in love and in all the ways adults can find to express that to one another, and how, despite all the odds against it, it's possible to find a happily every after!

I hope you'll have a chance to drop me a line: katerichards09@gmail.com or friend me on Facebook and let me know what you think about Terci and her Mistress's new life together.

Thanks once again and happy reading!

Kate

## Also by Kate Richards

*One Night on the Beach*

*Avalon for Christmas*

*The Virgin and the Playboy*

*The Virgin and the Best Man*

*Two Men and a Virgin*

*Gale Force Passion*

*Trail of Hearts*

*Madame Eve's Gift*

*Two Men*

*Virgin Underground*

*Two Dads for Christmas*

*The Milkman Cometh*

*Frontier Inferno*

*Lily in Chains*